Gudgekin the Thistle Girl and Other Tales

With the same disarming and richly fanciful humor that delighted readers of his first collection of fairy tales, *Dragon, Dragon*, John Gardner once again departs into a magical and mysterious land, where anything can happen—but never as you might expect. This companion volume of four contemporary fairy tales introduces a whole new cast of characters—some sweet and lovable, others wily and wicked, but all richly entertaining.

JOHN GARDNER

GUDGEKIN
THE THISTLE GIRL
and Other Tales

Illustrated by Michael Sporn

ALFRED A. KNOPF ✦ NEW YORK

To Joel and Lucy

THIS IS A BORZOI BOOK PUBLISHED BY ALFRED A. KNOPF, INC.

Text Copyright © 1976 by Boskydell Artists Ltd. Illustrations Copyright © 1976 by Michael Sporn. All rights reserved under International and Pan-American Copyright Conventions. Published in the United States by Alfred A. Knopf, Inc., New York, and simultaneously in Canada by Random House of Canada Limited, Toronto. Distributed by Random House, Inc., New York. Library of Congress Cataloging in Publication Data. Gardner, John Champlin, 1933—Gudgekin, the thistle girl, and other tales. CONTENTS: Gudgekin, the thistle girl.—The griffin and the wise old philosopher.—The Shape-Shifters of Shorm.—The sea-gulls. 1. Fairy tales. [1. Fairy tales]. I. Title. PZ8. G216Gu [Fic] 76-4819 ISBN 0-394-83276-0 ISBN 0-394-93276-5 lib. bdg. Manufactured in the United States of America 0987654321

Contents

Gudgekin
the Thistle Girl

In a certain kingdom there lived a poor little thistle girl. What thistle girls did for a living—that is, what people did with thistles—is no longer known, but whatever the reason that people gathered thistles, she was one of those who did it. All day long, from well before sunrise until long after sunset, she wandered the countryside gathering thistles, pricking her fingers to the bone, piling the thistles into her enormous thistle sack and carrying them back to her stepmother. It was a bitter life, but she always made the best of it and never felt the least bit sorry for herself, only for the miseries of others. The girl's name was Gudgekin.

Alas! The stepmother was never satisfied. She was arrogant and fiercely competitive, and when she laid out her thistles in her market stall, she would rather be dead than suffer the humiliation of seeing that some other stall had more thistles than she had. No one ever did, but the fear preyed on her, and no matter how many sacks of thistles poor Gudgekin gathered, there were never enough to give the stepmother comfort. "You don't earn your keep," the stepmother would say, crossing her arms and closing them together like scissors. "If you don't bring more thistles tomorrow, it's away you must go to the Children's Home and good riddance!"

Poor Gudgekin. Every day she brought more than yesterday, but every night the same. "If you don't bring more thistles tomorrow, it's away to the Home with you." She worked feverishly, frantically, smiling through her tears, seizing the thistles by whichever end came first, but never to her stepmother's satisfaction. Thus she lived out her miserable childhood, blinded by burning tears and pink with thistle pricks, but viewing her existence in the best light possible. As she grew older she grew more and more beautiful, partly because she was always smiling and refused to pout, whatever the provocation; and soon she was as lovely as any princess.

One day her bad luck changed to good. As she was jerking a thistle from between two rocks, a small voice cried, "Stop! You're murdering my children!"

"I beg your pardon?" said the thistle girl. When she bent down she saw a beautiful little fairy in a long white and silver dress, hastily removing her children from their cradle, which was resting in the very thistle that Gudgekin had been pulling.

"Oh," said Gudgekin in great distress.

The fairy said nothing at first, hurrying back and

forth, carrying her children to the safety of the nearest rock. But then at last the fairy looked up and saw that Gudgekin was crying. "Well," she said. "What's this?"

"I'm sorry," said Gudgekin. "I always cry. It's because of the misery of others, primarily. I'm used to it."

"Primarily?" said the fairy and put her hands on her hips.

"Well," sniffled Gudgekin, "to tell the truth, I do sometimes imagine I'm not as happy as I might be. It's shameful, I know. Everyone's miserable, and it's wrong of me to whimper."

"Everyone?" said the fairy, "—miserable? Sooner or later an opinion like that will make a fool of you!"

"Well, I really don't know," said Gudgekin, somewhat confused. "I've seen very little of the world, I'm afraid."

"I see," said the fairy thoughtfully, lips pursed. "Well, that's a pity, but it's easily fixed. Since you've spared my children and taken pity on my lot, I think I should do you a good turn."

She struck the rock three times with a tiny golden straw, and instantly all the thistles for miles around began moving as if by their own volition toward the thistle girl's sack. It was the kingdom of fairies, and the beautiful fairy with whom Gudgekin had made friends was none other than the fairies' queen. Soon the fairies had gathered all the thistles for a mile around, and had filled the sack that Gudgekin had brought, and had also filled forty-three more, which they'd fashioned on the spot out of gossamer.

"Now," said the queen, "it's time that you saw the world."

Immediately the fairies set to work all together and built a beautiful chariot as light as the wind, all transparent gossamer woven like fine thread. The chariot was so light that it needed no horses but flew along over the ground by itself, except when it was anchored with a stone. Next they made the thistle girl a gown of woven gossamer so lovely that not even the queen of the kingdom had anything to rival it; indeed, no one anywhere in the world had such a gown or has ever had, even to this day. For Gudgekin's head the fairies fashioned a flowing veil as light and silvery as the lightest, most silvery of clouds, and they sprinkled both the veil and the gown with dew so they glittered as if with costly jewels.

Then, to a tinny little trumpeting noise, the queen of the fairies stepped into the chariot and graciously held out her tiny hand to the thistle girl.

No sooner was Gudgekin seated beside the queen than the chariot lifted into the air lightly, like a swift little boat, and skimmed the tops of the fields and flew away to the capital.

When they came to the city, little Gudgekin could

scarcely believe her eyes. But there was no time to look at the curious shops or watch the happy promenading of the wealthy. They were going to the palace, the fairy queen said, and soon the chariot had arrived there.

It was the day of the kingdom's royal ball, and the chariot was just in time. "I'll wait here," said the kindly queen of the fairies. "You run along and enjoy yourself, my dear."

Happy Gudgekin! Everyone was awed by her lovely gown and veil; and even the fact that the fairies had neglected to make shoes for her feet, since they themselves wore none, turned out to be to Gudgekin's advantage. Barefoot dancing immediately became all the rage at court, and people who'd been wearing fine shoes for years slipped over to the window and slyly tossed them out, not to be outdone by a stranger. The thistle girl danced with the prince himself, and he was charmed more than words can tell. His smile seemed all openness and innocence, yet Gudgekin had a feeling he was watching her like a hawk. He had a reputation throughout the nine kingdoms for subtlety and shrewdness.

When it was time to take the thistle sacks back to her cruel stepmother, Gudgekin slipped out, unnoticed by anyone, and away she rode in the chariot.

"Well, how was it?" asked the queen of the fairies happily.

"Wonderful! Wonderful!" Gudgekin replied. "Except I couldn't help but notice how gloomy people were, despite their merry chatter. How sadly they frown when they look into their mirrors, fixing their make-up. Some of them frown because their feet hurt, I suppose; some of them perhaps because they're jealous of someone; and some of them perhaps because they've lost their youthful beauty. I could have wept for them!"

The queen of the fairies frowned pensively. "You're a good-hearted child, that's clear," she said, and fell silent.

They reached the field, and the thistle girl, assisted by a thousand fairies, carried her forty-four sacks to her wicked stepmother. The stepmother was amazed to see so many thistle sacks, especially since some of them seemed to be coming to the door all by themselves. Nevertheless, she said—for her fear of humiliation so drove her that she was never satisfied—"A paltry forty-four, Gudgekin! If you don't bring more thistles tomorrow, it's away to the Home with you!"

Little Gudgekin bowed humbly, sighed with resignation, forced to her lips a happy smile, ate her bread crusts, and climbed up the ladder to her bed of straw.

The next morning when she got to the field, she found eighty-eight thistle sacks stuffed full and waiting. The gossamer chariot was standing at anchor, and

the gossamer gown and veil were laid out on a rock, gleaming in the sun.

"Today," said the queen of the fairies, "we're going on a hunt."

They stepped into the chariot and flew off light as moonbeams to the royal park, and there, sure enough, were huntsmen waiting, and huntswomen beside them, all dressed in black riding-pants and riding-skirts and bright red jackets. The fairies made the thistle girl a gossamer horse that would sail wherever the wind might blow, and the people all said she was the most beautiful maiden in the kingdom, possibly an elf queen. Then the French horns and bugles blew, and the huntsmen were off. Light as a feather went the thistle girl, and the prince was so entranced he was beside himself, though he watched her, for all that, with what seemed to her a crafty smile. All too soon came the time to carry the thistle sacks home, and the thistle girl slipped from the crowd, unnoticed, and rode her light horse beside the chariot where the queen of the fairies sat beaming like a mother.

"Well," called the queen of the fairies, "how was it?"

"Wonderful!" cried Gudgekin, "it was truly wonderful! I noticed one thing, though. It's terrible for the fox!"

The queen of the fairies thought about it. "Blood sports," she said thoughtfully, and nodded. After that, all the rest of the way home, she spoke not a word.

When the thistle girl arrived at her stepmother's house, her stepmother threw up her arms in amazement at sight of those eighty-eight thistle-filled sacks. Nonetheless, she said as sternly as possible, "Eighty-eight! Why not a hundred? If you don't bring in more sacks tomorrow, it's the Home for you for sure!"

Gudgekin sighed, ate her dry crusts, forced a smile to her lips, and climbed the ladder.

The next day was a Sunday, but Gudgekin the thistle girl had to work just the same, for her stepmother's evil disposition knew no bounds. When she got to the field, there stood two times eighty-eight thistle sacks, stuffed to the tops and waiting. "*That* ought to fix her," said the queen of the fairies merrily. "Jump into your dress."

"Where are we going?" asked Gudgekin, as happy as could be.

"Why, to church, of course!" said the queen of the fairies. "After church we go to the royal picnic, and then we dance on the bank of the river until twilight."

"Wonderful!" said the thistle girl, and away they flew.

The singing in church was thrilling, and the sermon filled her heart with such kindly feelings toward her friends and neighbors that she felt close to dissolving in tears. The picnic was the sunniest in the history of the kingdom, and the dancing beside the river was delightful beyond words. Throughout it all the prince was beside himself with pleasure, never removing his eyes from Gudgekin, for he thought her the loveliest maiden he'd met in his life. For all his shrewdness, for all his aloofness and princely self-respect, when he danced with Gudgekin in her bejeweled gown of gossamer, it was all he could do to keep himself from asking her to marry him on the spot. He asked instead, "Beautiful stranger, permit me to ask you your name."

"It's Gudgekin," she said, smiling shyly and glancing at his eyes.

He didn't believe her.

"Really," she said, "it's Gudgekin." Only now did it strike her that the name was rather odd.

"Listen," said the prince with a laugh, "I'm *serious.* What is it really?"

"I'm serious too," said Gudgekin bridling. "It's Gudgekin the Thistle Girl. With the help of the fairies I've been known to collect two times eighty-eight sacks of thistles in a single day."

The prince laughed more merrily than ever at that. "Please," he said, "don't tease me, dear friend! A beautiful maiden like you must have a name like bells on Easter morning, or like songbirds in the meadow, or children's laughing voices on the playground! Tell me now. Tell me the truth. What's your name?"

"Puddin Tane," she said angrily, and ran away weeping to the chariot.

"Well," said the queen of the fairies, "how was it?"

"Horrible," snapped Gudgekin.

"Ah!" said the queen. "Now we're getting there!"

She was gone before the prince was aware that she was leaving, and even if he'd tried to follow her, the gossamer chariot was too fast, for it skimmed along like wind. Nevertheless, he was resolved to find and marry Gudgekin—he'd realized by now that Gudgekin must indeed be her name. He could easily understand the thistle girl's anger. He'd have felt the same himself, for he was a prince and knew better than anyone what pride was, and the shame of being made to seem a fool. He advertised far and wide for information on Gudgekin the Thistle Girl, and soon the news of the prince's search reached Gudgekin's cruel stepmother in her cottage. She was at once so furious she could hardly see, for she always wished evil for others and happiness for herself.

"I'll never in this world let him find her," thought the wicked stepmother, and she called in Gudgekin and put a spell on her, for the stepmother was a witch. She made Gudgekin believe that her name was Rosemarie and sent the poor baffled child off to the Children's Home. Then the cruel stepmother changed herself, by salves and charms, into a beautiful young

maiden who looked exactly like Gudgekin, and she set off for the palace to meet the prince.

"Gudgekin!" cried the prince and leaped forward and embraced her. "I've been looking for you everywhere to implore you to forgive me and be my bride!"

"Dearest prince," said the stepmother disguised as Gudgekin, "I'll do so gladly!"

"Then you've forgiven me already, my love?" said the prince. He was surprised, in fact, for it had seemed to him that Gudgekin was a touch more sensitive than that and had more personal pride. He'd thought, in fact, he'd have a devil of a time, considering how he'd hurt her and made a joke of her name. "Then you really forgive me?" asked the prince.

The stepmother looked slightly confused for an instant but quickly smiled as Gudgekin might have smiled and said, "Prince, I forgive you everything!" And so, though the prince felt queer about it, the day of the wedding was set.

A week before the wedding, the prince asked thoughtfully, "Is it true that you can gather, with the help of the fairies, two times eighty-eight thistle sacks all in one day?"

"Haven't I told you so?" asked the stepmother disguised as Gudgekin and gave a little laugh. She had a feeling she was in for it.

"You did say that, yes," the prince said, pulling with

two fingers at his beard. "I'd surely like to see it!"

"Well," said the stepmother, and curtsied, "I'll come to you tomorrow and you shall see what you shall see."

The next morning she dragged out two times eighty-eight thistle sacks, thinking she could gather in the thistles by black magic. But the magic of the fairies was stronger than any witch's, and since they lived in the thistles, they resisted all her fiercest efforts. When it was late afternoon the stepmother realized she had only one hope: she must get the real Gudgekin from the Children's Home and make her help.

Alas for the wicked stepmother, Gudgekin was no longer an innocent simpleton! As soon as she was changed back from simple Rosemarie, she remembered everything and wouldn't touch a thistle with an iron glove. Neither would she help her stepmother now, on account of all the woman's cruelty before, nor would she do anything under heaven that might be pleasing to the prince, for she considered him cold-hearted and inconsiderate. The stepmother went back to the palace empty-handed, weeping and moaning and making a hundred excuses, but the scales had now fallen from the prince's eyes—his reputation for shrewdness was in fact well founded—and after talking with his friends and advisers, he threw her in the dungeon. In less than a week her life in the dungeon was so miserable it made her repent and become a good woman, and the prince released her. "Hold your head high," he said, brushing a tear from his eye, for she made him think of Gudgekin. "People may speak of you as someone who's been in prison, but you're a better person now than before." She blessed him and thanked him and went her way.

Then once more he advertised far and wide through the kingdom, begging the real Gudgekin to forgive him and come to the palace.

"Never!" thought Gudgekin bitterly, for the fairy queen had taught her the importance of self-respect, and the prince's offense still rankled.

The prince mused and waited, and he began to feel a little hurt himself. He was a prince, after all, handsome and famous for his subtlety and shrewdness, and she was a mere thistle girl. Yet for all his beloved Gudgekin cared, he might as well have been born in some filthy cattle shed! At last he understood how things were, and the truth amazed him.

Now word went far and wide through the kingdom that the handsome prince had fallen ill for sorrow and was lying in his bed, near death's door. When the queen of the fairies heard the dreadful news, she was dismayed and wept tears of remorse, for it was all, she imagined, her fault. She threw herself down on the ground and began wailing, and all the fairies everywhere began at once to wail with her, rolling on the ground, for it seemed that she would die. And one of them, it happened, was living among the flowerpots in the bedroom of cruel little Gudgekin.

When Gudgekin heard the tiny forlorn voice wailing, she hunted through the flowers and found the fairy and said, "What in heaven's name is the matter, little friend?"

"Ah, dear Gudgekin," wailed the fairy, "our queen is dying, and if she dies we will all die of sympathy, and that will be that."

"Oh, you mustn't!" cried Gudgekin, and tears filled her eyes. "Take me to the queen at once, little friend, for she did a favor for me and I see I must return it if I possibly can!"

When they came to the queen of the fairies, the queen said, "Nothing will save me except possibly this, my dear: ride with me one last time in the gossamer chariot for a visit to the prince."

"Never!" said Gudgekin, but seeing the heartbroken looks of the fairies, she instantly relented.

The chariot was brought out from its secret place, and the gossamer horse was hitched to it to give it more dignity, and along they went skimming like wind until they had arrived at the dim and gloomy sickroom. The prince lay on his bed so pale of cheek and so horribly disheveled that Gudgekin didn't know him.

If he seemed to her a stranger it was hardly surprising; he'd lost all signs of his princeliness and lay there with his nightcap on sideways and he even had his shoes on.

"What's this?" whispered Gudgekin. "What's happened to the music and dancing and the smiling courtiers? And where is the prince?"

"Woe is me," said the ghastly white figure on the bed. "I was once that proud, shrewd prince you know, and this is what's become of me. For I hurt the feelings of the beautiful Gudgekin, whom I've given my heart and who refuses to forgive me for my insult, such is her pride and uncommon self-respect."

"My poor beloved prince!" cried Gudgekin when she heard this, and burst into a shower of tears. "You have given your heart to a fool, I see now, for I am your Gudgekin, simple-minded as a bird! First I had pity for everyone but myself, and then I had pity for no one but myself, and now I pity all of us in this miserable world, but I see by the whiteness of your cheeks that I've learned too late!" And she fell upon his bosom and wept.

"You give me your love and forgiveness forever and will never take them back?" asked the poor prince feebly, and coughed.

"I do," sobbed Gudgekin, pressing his frail, limp hand in both of hers.

"Cross your heart?" he said.

"Oh, I do, I *do!*"

The prince jumped out of bed with all his wrinkled clothes on and wiped the thick layer of white powder off his face and seized his dearest Gudgekin by the waist and danced around the room with her. The queen of the fairies laughed like silver bells and immediately felt improved. "Why you fox!" she told the prince. All the happy fairies began dancing with the prince and Gudgekin, who waltzed with her mouth open. When she closed it at last it was to pout, profoundly offended.

"Tr-tr-*tricked!*" she spluttered.

"Silly goose," said the prince, and kissed away the pout. "It's true, I've tricked you, I'm not miserable at all. But you've promised to love me and never take it back. My advice to you is, make the best of it!" He snatched a glass of wine from the dresser as he merrily waltzed her past, and cried out gaily, "As for myself, though, I make no bones about it: I intend to watch out for witches and live happily ever after. You must too, my Gudgekin! Cross your heart!"

"Oh, very well," she said finally, and let a little smile out. "It's no worse than the thistles."

And so they did.

The Griffin and the
Wise Old Philosopher

In a certain kingdom there lived a griffin. He was, like all griffins, a puzzle and an annoyance, and he had, like most griffins, the head and wings of an eagle and the body of a lion, or at least that was usually the case. Griffins are, above all, undependable. He was not, in all fairness, the worst kind of monster that a kingdom might be plagued by: he did not eat children—or anyone else, for that matter—in the way some griffins are purported to do; he was not slovenly or crass in his personal habits. All he did, in fact, was spread consternation and confusion wherever he appeared.

An electrician, for example, might be repairing an electric clock, a thing he'd done a thousand times and more, and suddenly there would be the griffin standing there, watching him with interest—not talking distractingly in his creaky, half-parrot, half-oldwomanish voice, and not soundlessly pacing on his large lion feet—doing nothing, in fact, absolutely nothing, and yet suddenly the old electrician would squint and purse his lips and, after a moment, take his glasses off, and he would look at the small, colored wires in his two hands, and for all his training and experience, would have no more idea which wire went where than would a camel. "*You*, griffin!" he would say, or he might even be so confused he couldn't think of the word *griffin*. "Haw *haw!*" the griffin would say, richly amused and profoundly disgusted by the stupidity of mankind, and would stride away. His going away would be no help, for that day at least, to the electrician. The day was ruined.

Or an experienced mason might be putting up a wall for a Sunday school, his assistant standing over by the mortar-mixing trough, sloshing the cement and sand and water back and forth, keeping them well mixed, and the griffin would appear, maybe ten feet away, lying in the grass like a cat, wings folded along his back, beaked head lifted, his beady black eyes watching with sober curiosity, and suddenly, for all his experience and training, the mason would find himself studying a question that had never gotten into his head before: "Which side of a brick is *up* and which side *down?*" A lunatic question you may say, and so it is, for the top and bottom of a brick are as identical as the mirror-image of a chicken and the chicken looking in at it. Nevertheless, the mason in his sudden bafflement could do nothing more about that wall until the question was settled in his mind, and the longer and harder he looked at that brick, the more certain he would grow that the brick's top and bottom were impossible to tell apart, so there was no way on earth he could be certain that the top was the top, and the bottom the bottom, and in his fury and frustration he would burst out crying. Meanwhile his assistant would have wandered off, forgetting he was part of the job, imagining he'd merely stopped to observe for a moment, as people all do when there's construction underway.

The griffin might materialize anywhere at all, sometimes by casually walking through a door or flying through a window, sometimes right out of thin air, since the griffin knew magic. He might materialize, wearing a black bow tie and sporting an expensive ivory-headed cane, at a concert of the Royal Symphony, when the king and queen themselves were in the royal box, and the French horns would all at once for no reason lose their count and come in seven measures early, or the oboe would go unaccountably flat, and everyone would suddenly be on a different page, some of them blasting out with all their might, some of them playing pianissimo. "Haw!" the griffin would remark and would walk out in disgust. The griffin had, in fact, the lowest possible opinion of people, though they somewhat amused him. Since everywhere he went he immediately caused confusion— since he'd never seen efficiency in anyone but himself —it seemed to the griffin that stupidity and befuddlement were the essence of human nature, though not of *his* nature. Undependable and changeable as he was, sometimes having three legs and sometimes four, sometimes believing *x* and sometimes vehemently denying *x*, he was nevertheless efficient at everything he did, with one exception, as you shall hear.

Observing the consistent stupidity of human nature, the griffin grew arrogant. In his travels to and fro, he was puzzled and confounded by nothing whatever in the world except—suddenly one day, when it dawned on him—the fact that somehow, when he wasn't there to watch, human beings *did*, occasionally, seem to get things done. Though he scorned human beings— hardly cared, in fact, whether they lived or died—this riddle began to pester him. How was it possible that creatures incapable of doing anything sometimes, nonetheless, *did* things? He would sit in his castle near the top of the mountain overlooking the kingdom, and would turn the question this way and that, upside and downside, the way the mason turned his brick, and after a while the griffin would grow downright cantankerous with frustration, though it did him no good. At last, eyes flashing with annoyance, he would fly back down to have a look at the people again, trying to catch them off guard. It of course never worked. He grew increasingly persistent, popping up everywhere, at all hours of the day and night. Soon all the trains

and planes and buses were hopelessly off schedule (many of them were lost, buses coming into their stations in the wrong cities or meandering down dirt roads or into farmers' yards, planes roaring north when they were supposed to roar south and ending up landing on some ice floe, the crew and passengers shivering and stamping their feet). There wasn't a bank in all the kingdom that knew how much money it had or ought to have, if any, and how much had been lost or misplaced in the computer, which seemed to have gone hopelessly insane.

"Who," said the king, who had called all his people to his palace in the village of Heizenburg, at the foot of Griffin's Mountain, "will rid me of this damnable griffin?"

No sooner had he asked the question than there stood the griffin, gazing out from beside the royal throne like an overgrown dog, surveying the crowd with furiously attentive eyes. Everyone began to think one thing and another, all of it wrong, and one by one they began to wander off, the griffin following, disappointed as usual, until no one was left but the king himself and one old man, a stout, white-bearded philosopher who was said to be wise, who had stayed up late reading the night before, and was now fast asleep on his feet.

"You, sir!" said the king.

The wise old philosopher blinked and gave his head a little shake and woke up. "Your highness?" he said, not quite certain where he was.

"You are willing to volunteer, then, to rid me of this griffin?"

"That," said the philosopher, "could be a difficult task."

"Never mind," said the king, "we'll pay you well. I will give you my daughter's hand in marriage and half the kingdom as her dowry."

"That won't be necessary," said the philosopher. "I'm an old man, and though I'm poor, I grant you, I'm used to it and fully content."

"You mean you'll rid me of this griffin for nothing?"

"Perhaps you could let me have a book or two," said the wise old philosopher, gazing up thoughtfully at the king's forehead, "or perhaps a supply of pencils, the kind with the pinched-flat erasers, if you know what I mean."

"I'll give you a truckload of books, my man, and a railroad car filled with pencils with pinched-flat erasers."

The philosopher sighed. Everyone was always getting carried away. What would he do with a railroad car filled with pencils, and where would anyone find a whole truckload of books worth reading? Well, that was life.

"Come to me again in three days," said the king, "and listen well: if you haven't gotten rid of the griffin, I'll throw you in jail."

The philosopher nodded and, profoundly, sighed again. He put his cap on and went out to the street and, thinking back carefully, remembered where his home was and, after making some calculations, drawing invisible numbers or else letters or possibly pictures on his left palm with his right forefinger, chose a path and went there.

His wife was an old battle-ax, or talked like one, though she loved him dearly, for they'd been married many years and understood each other. "And where have you been?" she said.

"I've been with the king," he said. "He offered me the princess and half the kingdom, but I told him no."

"Eh, you blockhead!" said his wife, "you might at least have taken his offer of half the kingdom. Look at this hovel we have to live in!"

"What would we have done with half the kingdom?"

"We could have rented it out, fool."

"That's true," he said, and sighed more profoundly than ever. "No matter; to get it I'd have had to rid the kingdom of the griffin—which, come to think of it, I have to do anyway, more's the pity—and if I haven't gotten rid of him in just three days, the king's going to throw me in his jail." He rolled his eyes up sadly. "I hope you'll visit."

"Don't count on it," she said. However, she patted his arm and took his elbow, leading him to the kitchen. "Come and eat your supper."

Wise or not, the stout, white-bearded old philosopher had no idea how to get rid of the griffin. There were no books on the subject, and so far as he could figure, the problem had no rational solution. He went for a walk and his old wife went with him, carrying the lunch basket, and they walked all day except for lunchtime, but the philosopher could think of nothing and at last went back home. "If you're so wise, old dolt," said the philosopher's wife when they'd finished eating supper, "it seems to me you'd think of some idea."

"I know," said the philosopher, "but it's not the way I work. I always start with the assumption that I know nothing, and probably nobody else knows much either, however they may prattle and labor to sound convincing."

"Nonsense," said the wife. "You know the world is round. You know oysters don't wear shoes."

"That's true," said the philosopher. "You see? I was wrong again."

"Well, old miserable blockhead that you are," said

the philosopher's wife, not meaning it unkindly, "you're better off than some. A griffin doesn't change your way of thinking."

"That's an interesting point," said the philosopher, thoughtfully squinting and pulling at his beard. "It's a point that may well prove useful, if I can manage to remember it." Then he kissed his old wife fondly and they went up to bed.

Meanwhile the griffin had been up to his usual mischief. He visited the Post Office and the mailmen became so befuddled and confounded that they ended up feeding all the letters to the bears at the zoo. He visited the village's Catholic church, and the priest became so mixed up he converted the congregation to Judaism. He visited the county library and so confused the librarians that when he left, *The Five Little Peppers* was under home economics.

So the first day was over, and the philosopher had two days left.

The second day the old philosopher decided, using a technique that had proved useful sometimes, that perhaps the reason he couldn't answer his question was that he was asking the wrong question. Instead of asking himself, as he'd been doing so far, "How the devil does a person make a griffin go away?" he decided he would ask, "Is a red fire engine red inherently or by definition?" To work on this problem, he went

for a walk with his old wife. As before, they carried a lunch basket, or rather she carried it, since she was stronger. They walked all day, except for an hour or so at lunchtime, the old philosopher lost in thought, his old wife muttering to herself and occasionally stooping down to pick a daisy, careful not to bother her old husband. When it was beginning to get dark they went home to have their supper, and after they had eaten it the wife asked, "Well, have you figured it out yet?"

"Tentatively at least," said the philosopher. "Red fire engines are red by definition."

"No, blockhead," she said, "have you figured out how to drive off the griffin?"

"Ah, that," said the philosopher. "Perhaps I could just go talk to him. Why should a griffin be unreasonable?"

"By definition, lummox," said his wife.

"Hmm," said the old philosopher, frowning thoughtfully. "That's very interesting! That's a very interesting point indeed and may prove useful, one way or another, if I can just somehow keep it in mind."

That day, once again, the griffin had been everywhere, making life in the kingdom so miserable that nothing was accomplished. There were farmers up sitting on the peaks of their barns, no one could say why; there were fishermen boring holes in trees; a local jeweler with an excellent reputation spent the whole day painting six parsnips bright green. The griffin, looking at all this, tipped his head as a chicken might do, or a robin listening for worms as it walks on a lawn. At the end of the day, when the philosopher and his wife were trudging home, the griffin walked with scornful dignity on silent catpaws up the mountain to his castle, pausing only once to look back at the village at the foot of the mountain. The griffin once again tipped his eagle head, baffled, and watched for a moment with his bright black eagle eye for some sign, *any* sign, of meaningful activity down below. But nothing was happening, or nothing but the day's lingering confusion, and the griffin, in great perplexity, shook his head and continued up the mountain.

So the second day ended, and the philosopher had one day left. This third day he got a sack lunch from his wife and went out of the house alone, for though the idea was depressing to him, he had decided to go reason with the griffin. As he climbed the mountain he analyzed his conundrum from various points of view, and if one thing struck him more forcefully than another, it was this: following out to their logical conclusions his thoughts (insofar as he remembered them) of the previous two days, he would have to say (he thought) that he had in this griffin business a distinct advantage over other men, in that a man utterly confused from the start cannot have his thinking significantly altered by the appearance of a griffin. But though professionally confused—confused, that is, by inclination and training—he was no better off than an ordinary man whom a griffin is visiting when it came to understanding a griffin, since a griffin is by definition unreasonable. Nevertheless the old man trudged on, helping himself up the mountain with his cane, and came at last to the castle. It was a splendid castle, but the old man, wandering through it, hardly noticed, for he was lost in thought as usual, and when he found the griffin on his high golden throne he was as befuddled as an ordinary man would be, for a curious problem was molesting his thoughts: what about red fire engines repainted blue? All this he explained to the griffin—or whomever—for he hardly paid attention, and the griffin—or whoever—stared at him as he would at a madman, and at last, with a sigh, the old philosopher went home.

"Old blockhead," said his wife, meeting him at the door to invite him to supper, "here it is practically dark on the third day, and you haven't solved the problem. You poor dunce, now you'll have to go to jail."

"But I *have* solved the problem," said the philosopher, looking up innocently, "and right after supper we'll walk over and speak with the king."

"You have?" said his wife, and her eyes widened—

though she'd known him for too many years ever to doubt that he would solve it. "Well bless my soul but you're a wise one, as I've always maintained!" They ate their supper and, after it was over, put on their good clothes and set out, holding hands like two simpletons, for the royal palace.

Meanwhile the griffin spent another busy day. Not a jot or tittle of work got done anywhere, for whenever a carpenter began hammering a nail, there the griffin would be, and the carpenter would fall into rudimentary doubts, wondering, for example, why he'd chosen nails instead of wooden pegs, or then again, Lucite; and whenever the man on the ferryboat got set to travel from the left bank to the right, there would be the griffin, sitting on the pilothouse, and the man would at once begin to question in his heart whether one end of the ferry or the other could be called, technically, the front end, and if so, whether or not he was going backwards, and wondering, moreover, in what sense, if any, it could be seriously maintained that one side of the river, and not the other, was really the *left* side. These inquiries so troubled him that in the end he merely sat in the exact middle of the river, with his head in his hands and the sweat pouring down off his forehead, and thought and thought. In the middle of that afternoon the griffin, while walking through a schoolroom, abruptly frowned, his eagle head cocked sharply, and reflected, "For three days I've been watching these people steadily and like a hawk, trying to find out how it is that though they never succeed at doing anything, they manage to get things done; and for three days I have seen, by unmistakable evidence, that in fact they do *not* get anything done. It was clearly an illusion, when it seemed to me before that they did get things done. Now that that's settled, why am I wasting my time with these fools, since they no longer even amuse me any more? I will go back to my castle and never again waste my head on them." And he flew out the schoolroom window and straight to his castle, which he never left again in all his life.

Meanwhile the wise old philosopher and his wife were standing before the king's throne, and the king had called in all his servants and a great crowd of citizens from the street, for this was a great occasion, at least in the king's mind, though the philosopher, standing with his arms folded over his great white beard and his head tipped forward, his spectacles fallen to the tip of his nose, was beginning to drift off.

At last, in a booming voice that woke the philosopher, the king said, "Well, old philosopher, have you rid me of that griffin?"

"Let me understand this," the philosopher said. "Whenever people see the griffin, they immediately become utterly befuddled, so they don't know anything at all. Is that so?"

"Certainly that's so," said the king. "Everyone knows that."

"They aren't sure of *anything*?" inquired the philosopher.

"Nothing," snapped the king impatiently. "Get to the point. Have you rid me of the griffin or haven't you?"

"What griffin?" asked the wise old philosopher.

All the people were shocked. The king was furious. But in the days that followed, as the kingdom gradually came back to proper order, and no one felt confused—except, as usual, the philosopher—it was seen that the wise old philosopher was right as rain.

The Shape-Shifters
of Shorm

They were known as the terrible Shape-Shifters of Shorm, and whenever their name was mentioned even the emperor himself went deathly pale, and rightly. For a man might be walking the road at dusk, speaking casually of this and that with a man he had met that day in town—some kind old peasant with a gentle face, or some traveling tinker with stories to tell, some friendly creature who would never harm a fly—and suddenly, quick as the blink of an eye, the stranger might stand transformed to, for instance, an owl. It was unnatural, illogical, a violation of order- -though the shape-shifters, it is true, did no one any damage.

The emperor sent out an urgent call for aid through the whole of the empire, and he swore that the person who could cleanse the empire of the terrible shape-shifters would have as his reward whatever he dared to name.

Now in a certain village there lived a woodchopper who had grown too old and feeble to chop wood. Everyone knew him as a troublesome fellow, unpredictable and cranky. When people tried to reason with him, all the old woodchopper would say was "Bah!" When they tried to organize some community effort, the woodchopper would lock his doors and refuse to come out.

On the day the emperor's proclamation was nailed up, the woodchopper was sitting with his ax on the curbstone, peacefully thinking about the good old days, chopping down trees and occasionally slicing off the head of a wolf; but sunk in thought as he was, he couldn't help but notice the proclamation being posted and the people all gathering to read it. After a while, against his better judgment, he went over to look at it too.

All the people were saying excitedly, "Any reward a man dares to name! Think of it!" They were all eager to be off to the imperial palace.

But the woodchopper merely pursed his lips and read the proclamation three times, carefully, running his finger along beneath the words. "Bah, there's got to be a catch," he said at last, and he went back over to the curbstone and sat down.

"What catch?" the people all said angrily. "How could there possibly be a catch? It's from the emperor himself. Don't you believe in *anything*?"

"We'll see," the woodchopper said. "How are you going to tell the shape-shifters from ordinary people? False arrest is a serious business."

But he was talking to himself, for by now everybody in the village had gone to the imperial palace. Or, rather, everybody but the woodchopper and two old hags who were beating an ox with a long, thick stick.

Meanwhile, at the imperial palace, the emperor watched all the people gathering, and he was pleased with the turnout. They came from the farthest corners of the empire—knights and dukes, wizards, scholars, housewives, adventurers, hucksters, tailors—and the palace was packed so full there was nowhere more to stand. "Welcome!" cried the emperor, clapping his hands with pleasure. "Welcome one and all!"

Now the first to offer his services was a humpbacked knight dressed in scarlet. "If I rid the empire of the shape-shifters, Your Imperial Majesty," the knight said slyly, "I ask one half of the empire as my prize."

The people all widened their eyes a little, startled that he should ask for so much. You could have heard a pin drop. But then the emperor said, "Done!"—a little crossly—and it was settled.

So the humpbacked knight in scarlet set out from the palace and said he'd return by the first day's sunrise. However, he didn't return. A hush fell over the great crowd waiting at the palace gates, and they watched the sun rise higher and higher, and some said, "He'll come yet," and some said, "Never." And then it was noon, and they knew that the knight wouldn't make it.

Meanwhile, the feeble old woodchopper was sitting on the curbstone, at home in his village with his ax beside him, watching the two old hags beating their ox. He watched for a long time, having nothing to do, and after a while it occurred to him that maybe they were shape-shifters. Otherwise why hadn't they gone off to the palace with the rest? "But nothing's simple in this world," he thought, for he had no faith in logic. "There must be some catch." On second thought, though, he walked over closer, taking his ax, and stood watching them until sunset. Sure enough, just at sunset, the two old hags turned into oxen, and the ox turned into a hedgehog. Before they could run away the wood-chopper cut off their heads and stuffed them in a sack.

Now the woodchopper was the only one left in the village, so he decided to go to a neighboring village and see if there was anyone there who hadn't gone off to the palace with the others. There was no one there but a humpbacked knight in scarlet. The woodchopper shook his head and chuckled and said to himself, "There's got to be a catch." However, he cut off the knight's head and put it in his sack and hurried to the next town to see what was there.

Back at the palace, the second man to offer aid to the emperor was an ancient wizard all dressed in black. He said, "If I rid the empire of the shape-shifters, Your

Imperial Majesty, my reward shall be half the empire and your daughter's hand in marriage."

Again the people were dismayed by such boldness, but again the emperor, after swallowing twice, said "Done!" and the wizard rode off. He said he would return by the second day at sunrise, but he, too, was wrong. The sky grew light on the eastern horizon, and all the people came down to the palace and waited, and soon the rim of the sun appeared, and later the whole sun, and before long it was noon, and they knew the old wizard wouldn't make it.

The reason was that the woodchopper had met him, in the fourth village the woodchopper came to, where he'd also met five old men picking peppers, and sometimes as they reached out for the peppers their hands were paws, and sometimes they were hands, and sometimes hoofs. The woodchopper quickly cut off all their heads, including the wizard's, and stuffed them in his sack.

The third to offer his help to the emperor was a wrinkled old mechanic with tattoos on his shoulders and birthmarks even on his ears. He said he wanted the *whole* empire and the emperor's daughter's hand in marriage.

"That's a lot," said the emperor, with a look of indignation. However, after swallowing several times, he clenched his fists and accepted, for the sake of his dignity, because he'd promised.

So the mechanic went out, and he said he would be back by the third day's sunrise. But no one believed him, and when the third day's sunrise came, hardly anyone bothered to get up and watch for him. Sure enough, morning came as usual, but not the mechanic.

"That's life," said the people, for though they were optimists, they believed above all in regularity, and when two quests had failed they could easily predict, they thought, the third.

"Well," said the emperor, looking around despondently, "who's next?"

But nobody was eager to meet the challenge now. They said, "Your Imperial Majesty, there's something fishy going on around here. The Shape-Shifters of Shorm never used to hurt people, they just shape-shifted. It was annoying and alarming and unnatural, but it wasn't like *this*. In our opinion, you should have left well enough alone." The emperor flew into a rage, but secretly he agreed with them.

Just then who should appear at the palace gate but the woodchopper, dragging his huge sack of heads.

"Your Imperial Majesty," he said, "I've brought you the heads of the Shape-Shifters of Shorm. Is it true you'll give me whatever I dare to name?"

The emperor frowned. "What's the catch?" he said.

"No catch," the woodchopper said. "I just want to know the rules."

"Ask away," said the emperor. "You're among honorable men."

"All right," said the woodchopper. Then he said, not knowing how much the others had asked for, "I'd like a round-trip ticket to Brussels, to take a short vacation."

"Done," said the emperor quick as a flash, and the people all laughed and poked each other and pointed at the woodchopper and laughed some more, and then they looked inside the sack. Sure enough, there were all the shape-shifters' heads, and some of the time they were wolves' heads, and some of the time they were peacocks' heads, and some of the time they were oxen, and sometimes bears. But three of them, unluckily, were the knight, the wizard, and the mechanic.

"What's this?" cried the emperor. "Good heavens, this is murder! Guards! Guards!"

The guards came running, and the emperor said, "Put this man in the dungeon. Tomorrow he hangs!"

The woodchopper looked in the sack and now he noticed it too. He said, "Then I don't get my vacation?"

The emperor rubbed his chin. "Hmm," he said. After a long period of reflection he said, "You can go visit Brussels, but you have to wear handcuffs, and I'm

sending along guards. After you get back, you hang.
Do you solemnly swear you won't escape?"

"I swear," said the woodchopper.

The people all nodded and agreed it was fair.

So the poor old woodchopper traveled off to Brussels. When he'd been there three days, he suddenly bolted down an alley and escaped, and he changed his name to Zobrowski and dropped out of sight.

The Sea Gulls

A king was walking in the forest one day when a huge ogre saw him and picked him up in his hand. "What a tasty morsel," said the ogre, and prepared to eat him.

"Wait," said the king. "Let me offer you a bargain. We will play a game of chance. If you win you may eat me right now, and if *I* win, you may eat me and all my children in seven years." In seven years the king thought he could raise an army against the ogre and kill him and thus get out of his bargain.

"Fair enough," said the ogre. And they played a game of dice. The king, who was a cheater, won, and the ogre left the country for seven years.

The king was so pleased at having won that he promptly forgot all about his terrible bargain. But when the seven years were nearly up, he suddenly remembered the ogre and began to feel alarmed. He tried to raise an army to fight the ogre, but no one would have any part of it. Then, while the king was running around in his garden, not knowing which way to turn, he saw a woman up in a tree. She was a wicked witch.

"I will save you," said the witch, "if you will give me your three fat sons to feed my geese."

"I have a better idea," said the king. "Let us play a game of chance. If you win you may eat my sons, but if *I* win, then in seven years you may eat my three sons and myself and my daughter."

"They're not for *me*, they're for my geese," said the witch.

"Yes, that's what I meant to say," said the king.

The king smiled slyly, for in seven years he thought he could find a way to murder the wicked witch and get out of his bargain.

They rolled the dice and, cheating as usual, the king won, and immediately the wicked witch turned into an owl so large that her head was hidden in the clouds. When the ogre came, dressed in his finest, she ate him like a dumpling. Then the wicked witch vanished.

The king was so pleased with his good luck that he again forgot all about his bargain, and seven years passed as quickly as a day. Then the king happened to remember the wicked witch. He asked all his kingdom for advice, and this time there was no one at all who could help him.

Seeing that their father was at his wit's end, the king's three sons and daughter ran and hid in the woods. They met an old hermit with a tangled beard and a solid iron eye, and when they had told him their troubles the hermit said, "If you really wish to escape the wicked witch, the thing to do is turn into sea gulls and fly away."

"How do we do it?" cried the king's sons.

The hermit said, "You simply say:

> *Wind, wind, whither do you blow?*
> *Make me a gull for evermore.*

There's just one catch," said the hermit. "Not all the magic in Lapland can turn you back to children."

Just then they heard a horrible laugh: The wicked witch was coming. As fast as they could get the words out, the three brothers said,

> *Wind, wind, whither do you blow?*
> *Make me a gull for evermore.*

And they changed into sea gulls and flew away.

But the king's daughter would not change. "I would rather be eaten by a goose than turn into a sea gull forever," she said. "It might be all right for a little while, but forever is too long."

Suddenly the trees all around the king's daughter turned to gold, and where the old hermit had been standing there stood a handsome prince.

"Well I never!" cried the princess.

The prince explained that once, long since, the wicked witch had turned him into an old hermit, and the bargain was that he must remain a hermit until somewhere on earth he found someone with a proper sense of values—for instance, someone who knew that, whatever one might think at first glance, people are better than sea gulls. That had been years and years ago, and he'd begun to despair—until the princess came along.

Then the prince and the princess were married and moved to the prince's palace on a high cliff overlooking the ocean. All day and all night the princess's brothers, who were still sea gulls, flew high above the water, crying in an irritable voice, "Lost! Lost!" The princess visited them every day and made their lives as pleasant as she could by throwing them old bread crumbs. No one ever saw the king again. Most likely the wicked witch got him for gambling and scheming and weaseling out of his debts.

John Gardner's compelling and brilliant fiction—including *Nickel Mountain, The King's Indian,* and *Grendel*—has earned him a respected place as a major figure in contemporary American literature. When he first turned his pen to children's books with *Dragon, Dragon* (1975), his extraordinary—if irreverent—wit was broadly welcomed as a delightful addition to the storytelling genre.

Mr. Gardner, born in Batavia, New York, is on the faculty of Southern Illinois University, in Carbondale, Illinois. He has taught medieval literature and creative writing at a number of colleges and universities, and is now living in Vermont with his wife and two children.

Michael Sporn was born and raised in New York City. After receiving his degree in Fine Arts, he began work in film animation. His credits include the feature-length film *Raggedy Ann and Andy,* the Academy Award nominee "Voyage to Next," and numerous cartoons for *The Electric Company.* He has also begun illustrating for *The Electric Company Magazine.* This is his first book.

Mr. Sporn lives in Forest Hills, New York.